P9-DNH-215

GO FOR THE
GOAL!

FRED BOWEN
SPORTS STORY series

FRED BOWEN series
SPORTS STORY

GO FOR THE GOAL!

PEACHTREE
ATLANTA

Published by
PEACHTREE PUBLISHERS
1700 Chattahoochee Avenue
Atlanta, Georgia 30318-2112
www.peachtree-online.com

Text © 2012 by Fred Bowen

Cover design by Thomas Gonzalez and Maureen Withee
Book design by Melanie McMahon Ives

Printed in March 2012 in the United States of America by R.R. Donnelley and Sons, Harrisonburg, Virginia
10 9 8 7 6 5 4 3 2 1
First edition

Library of Congress Cataloging-in-Publication Data
    Bowen, Fred.
        Go for the goal! / Fred Bowen.
            p. cm.
        Summary: Thirteen-year-old Josh joins an elite travel league soccer team on which the individual members are all talented but not playing well as a team, so their coach suggests that they do some team-building exercises.
        ISBN 13: 978-1-56145-632-1 / ISBN 10: 1-56145-632-2
        [1. Soccer--Fiction. 2. Teamwork (Sports)--Fiction.] I. Title.
        PZ7.B6724Gnm 2012
        [Fic]--dc23
                                            2012004034

For everyone who works so hard to get books to kids—especially my friends at Turning the Page, First Book, and KPMG's Family for Literacy

Josh Bradshaw burst through the front door and scrambled upstairs. Aidan McFarland, Josh's best friend, was not far behind.

"Hey, keep it down," Josh's father called as the door slammed behind the boys. "I'm trying to work."

"It's just Aidan and me, Dad," Josh called back. "We're going to my room."

The two friends tossed their backpacks onto the bedroom floor, which was covered in dirty clothes and old school papers. "Man, carrying around all these books should get us in shape for soccer," Aidan said. He glanced at Josh and added, "Do you think it's on the website yet?"

"Coach Hodges said she would post the list of players who made the team on Monday," Josh said.

The boys smiled and sang out together: "And it's Monday!"

"Where's your laptop?" Aidan asked, looking around the room.

"I think it's on my bed somewhere." Josh pushed away the sheets. "Here it is." He flipped open his computer and took a deep breath.

"Why are you so nervous?" Aidan said, scooting onto the bed next to Josh. "We'll make it."

"I don't know," Josh said as he started tapping the keys. "There were a lot of good players at the tryouts. Coach can't keep everybody."

"Yeah, but you're the best scorer," Aidan insisted. "You must have scored a million goals for the Flames last year."

"Playing with a rec-league team like the Flames is different," Josh said. "The United's a travel team. They're like All-Stars."

"I know. That's why playing with the United will be so cool," Aidan said. "Everybody's good."

The United website popped up and the boys leaned closer. "Click on *News*," Aidan said.

"There it is!" Josh shouted as he read from the screen. "United Names U-14 Team." His heart jumped. He wasn't at all confident he had made it.

"Come on! Click it!" screamed Aidan.

"Okay, okay," Josh said. A list of names appeared.

UNITED ROSTER	
Evan Perry	Kadir Sims
Victor Baldassi	Aidan McFarland
Robert Brodie	Langston Adams
Dylan Cole	Demetrius Brown
Patrick West	Thomas Smythe
Joshua Bradshaw	Ty Robinson
Mario Barretto	Robin Hall
Noah Stern	Fletcher Downing
Paul Chambers	Walter Winwood

The room was quiet as the boys scanned the list. Then, at the same instant they shouted, "Yes! We made it!"

They jumped off the bed and bounced around the bedroom, bumping chests and throwing clothes into the air. "We are the United! We are the United! We are the United!" they chanted at the top of their lungs.

Mr. Bradshaw stuck his head into the room. "Keep it down, will you," he said sharply. "I told you I was—"

"We made it, Dad!" The words burst out of Josh. "The United! We made the team."

Mr. Bradshaw's head snapped back in surprise. "They've posted the roster already?"

Aidan turned the laptop around. "Take a look."

Josh's father leaned over the screen. A satisfied smile creased his face. "All right!" he said. "Congratulations!" He traded high fives with Josh and Aidan, then looked back at the screen. "Do you know any of these other guys?"

Josh and Aidan studied the roster.

"That guy Mario played in our league last year. He was good," Josh said. "We got Patrick West too. He's an awesome goalie."

"And we played against that kid, Kadir Sims, in rec league," Aidan said. "He was kind of a whiner. Always looking at the ref to call a penalty."

"Remember, we were playing *against* him," Josh said. "Now we're going to be playing *with* him."

Josh kept studying the roster. "Evan Perry. He was that kid with the fancy red shoes who played midfield during the scrimmages," Josh recalled. "He acted like he's the next Pelé or something."

"Someone said he played for the United last season," Aidan said. "He's good."

"Victor Baldassi played for the United last season too," Josh added. "I've heard about him. He's a terrific scorer." Josh smiled. "I can't believe we're going to be playing with these guys."

"Remember you two are as good as any of them," Mr. Bradshaw said. "Coach picked you because you could help the team."

Josh was quiet for a moment. He could feel a certain pride swelling up inside him. *I've always wanted to play on a really great team—a team like the United,* he thought. *And now I've got my chance.*

"When are practices?" his father asked.

"Tuesdays and Thursdays. I guess we start tomorrow."

"What about games?"

"Click on the schedules," Aidan said.

A list of dates and team names replaced the roster on the screen.

UNITED SCHEDULE

September 1	Labor Day Tournament	TBA
September 8	Tournament	TBA
September 15	Kings*	2 P.M.
September 22	Magic*	Noon
September 29	Storm*	10 A.M.
October 6	Red Devils*	Noon
October 13	Dynasty*	2 P.M.
October 20	Columbus Day Tournament	TBA
October 27	Future*	10 A.M.
November 3	Galaxy*	10 A.M.
November 10	Veterans Day Tournament	TBA
November 17	Majestics*	Noon
November 24	Arsenal*	2 P.M.
December 1	League Tournament	TBA
December 2	League Tournament	TBA

* League Games—All League Games will be played at the Soccerplex

"The ones with the stars are the league games," Josh explained. "Coach Hodges said we're going to play in a bunch of tournaments too."

"Where's the coach from?" Mr. Bradshaw asked.

Josh clicked a picture of Coach Hodges and read her biography. "She played four years at University of Notre Dame—"

"They're good," Aidan interrupted.

"She's been coaching the United for three years," Josh continued. "She's the real deal."

"Yeah, she seemed like she knew her stuff at the tryouts," Aidan said.

Josh clicked a small picture of last year's United team and it filled the screen.

"I love their uniforms!" Aidan shouted.

"You mean *our* uniforms," Josh corrected. "Hey look, there's Evan."

"Is he wearing red shoes?" Mr. Bradshaw asked.

Josh and Aidan laughed and then returned to surfing through the site, taking in everything—the schedules, the pictures, the uniforms—in almost reverent silence.

Finally, Josh turned and smiled at Aidan and his dad. "Playing for the United is going to be *so* cool!" he declared.

Chapter 2

Tweeeet! Coach Hodges blew her whistle long and loud. In midstride, the United players stopped their drills. "All right, water break," Coach announced.

"Finally," Josh said. The sweat was pouring down his face as he turned the tiny spigot at the bottom of the big orange jug and filled his water bottle. "This thing is so slow," he said, wiping his forehead with the back of his arm. Before the bottle was even half full, he yanked it back and took big grateful gulps.

"Move over," Aidan said, pushing his own bottle under the spigot.

Instead of drinking his water, Aidan dumped it over his head and let the cold water splash onto his sweaty hair and down his back. He wiped his mouth with his wet T-shirt. "Tough practice," he said in a low voice. "Especially for the first one."

"It's not too bad," Josh said. "It's just the heat. It's August. It's not going to be hot much longer."

Aidan looked over at Evan, who was in the water line. "Hey, Evan, are practices always going to be like this?"

"What do you mean?"

Josh picked up on Aidan's question. "You know, just drills. Not many breaks. It seems like Coach never lets up."

Evan shot a phony smile at the other United players in line and then said a little too loudly, "What's the matter? Can't you take it, rookie? This isn't rec league, you know." His teammates chuckled.

"We can take it," Josh answered, feeling annoyed. "We were just asking."

"If you can't take it," Evan continued, "Coach'll find somebody else. She got rid of two guys last year. Cut 'em after a couple practices."

"Really?" Aidan blurted out.

"Sure," Evan said, splashing some water on his face. "Coach is always looking to get better. Lots of guys want to play on the United."

Tweeeet!

"Okay, break's over. Let's hustle." Coach Hodges looked at her watch. "We have time for a quick scrimmage. Nine on nine. C'mon, let's go." She grabbed a handful of yellow mesh shirts and called out names for the two teams.

"Looks like we're on different teams," Aidan said as Josh pulled the yellow shirt over his head.

"Yeah, I get to play with Mr. Red Shoes," Josh said, eyeing Evan's fancy footwear.

"Lucky you," Aidan teased. "Watch out. He might make you kiss his shoes."

"Well, at least he can play," Josh said. "Did you see him in the drills? The guy's got some serious skills."

"So does everybody on this team. Victor. Kadir. Mario. Patrick. They all can play."

"That's why it's going to be so much better

than playing for the Flames," Josh said.

"Okay, let's get started!" Coach shouted. "I want to see some hustle."

Josh studied the two teams on the practice pitch. Neither team was stacked with the best players. *Looks like Coach Hodges hasn't picked the starting team yet,* he thought. *I better play well if I want to be a starter—or play at all.*

The scrimmage started fast. Evan chipped a ball into the offensive zone and Josh raced after it. A defender battled Josh with a grab at his shirt and an elbow to his ribs. Josh glanced at Coach Hodges, expecting a call.

"Play on!" she barked. "Come on, Josh, get some space!" Coach kept after him. "I thought you were fast. Use your speed."

Josh noticed the United scrimmage was faster, tougher, and much more competitive than the Flames rec-league games. *I gotta start dishing it out instead of just taking it,* he thought.

"Five more minutes," Coach called out to the team. "Let's see more ball movement, more passing."

Evan made a steal and dribbled upfield. Seeing an opening, Josh darted up the wing, stretching out his hand, trying to get Evan's attention. But Evan ignored him and kept charging forward.

Aidan stopped Evan with a perfect tackle and his team took possession.

Josh couldn't believe it. Maybe it was the heat, but he was getting tired of Evan hogging the ball. He turned and hustled back on defense. A few minutes later, the scrimmage ended. No goals. No more scoring chances.

"Good work, guys!" Coach Hodges shouted. "Not bad for a first practice. Especially in this weather."

"Any news about the tournaments?" Victor asked.

"Not yet. Don't worry. I'll e-mail everyone about the first tournament. See you Thursday."

The players headed straight for the water jug and one last cold drink. Aidan and Josh held back and let the others go first.

"We didn't look so great," Aidan said as he picked at his sweaty T-shirt to keep it from sticking to his skin.

"It's gonna take time," Josh said, using his own T-shirt to wipe his face. "It's just our first practice and it was super hot. We're not with the Flames anymore where we knew everybody. We gotta get used to these guys. Our timing was off."

"There was a lot of pushing and grabbing out there," Aidan said.

Josh laughed. "Maybe that's why our timing was off."

The players trudged through the steamy air and toward their parents, who waited in their air-conditioned cars.

"Hey, Evan," Josh called ahead to the United midfielder. "I thought you were going to pass me the ball on that play. I was open on the wing. Didn't you see me?"

Evan turned. He looked surprised. "Yeah, I saw you," he said. "But you didn't do much with the first ball I chipped to you. So why would I…"

Evan didn't finish his sentence. He got distracted when he spotted his dad waving and calling for him to hurry up.

Josh stopped short and shot a glance at Aidan.

"Ouch," Aidan said.

"What's with that guy?" Josh asked, his eyes blazing. "He acts like he owns the team."

Aidan threw his arm around his friend's shoulder and said, "I guess he's just saying, 'Welcome to the United.'"

Chapter 3

Josh could smell dinner cooking when he walked into the house after another United practice. His cleats clattered against the tile floor as he tossed his equipment bag near the back door.

"Josh, take off those shoes." Mr. Bradshaw was stirring a simmering pot on the stove. "Hey, how was practice today?"

"Okay."

"It was hot as blazes again out there," Mrs. Bradshaw complained as she followed Josh into kitchen. "I don't know how the kids stand it for two hours."

"It's tough, Mom, but Coach always gives us plenty of water breaks." Josh looked into the pot. "What's for dinner?"

"Chili. It'll be done in ten minutes."

"Traffic was awful," Mrs. Bradshaw said. "I wish the practices were closer." She looked over at Josh. "Is there anyone we can carpool with? It took forever again today."

"Not really. I still don't know anybody on the team that well. Except Aidan."

"Really?" his father said. He tossed a bag of tortilla chips on the table. "How many practices have you had?"

"Today was our fifth." He shrugged and started eating the chips. "I don't know, the guys on the team just aren't that friendly. Anyway, I don't think any of them live nearby. Plus we got two new kids today."

"Hey, Josh, give me some of those," his mother said, motioning for the bag.

"Two new kids? Don't you have a full squad?" his father asked.

"Coach cut two kids," Josh said.

"Really?"

"Yeah."

"I don't know why you have to play for this team," his mother said, taking a handful of chips and handing the bag back to Josh. "It seems to me the Flames were fine. And the practices were a lot closer."

"The United are much better than those guys. They're faster—got better skills. I have to play much harder to keep up. I'm getting a lot better already," Josh said.

"The Flames were a good team," Mrs. Bradshaw insisted. "You won almost all your games."

"That was just a rec league."

"And you've known some of those kids on the Flames, like Chris and Nick, since kindergarten," she reminded him.

"Yeah, but—"

"I think that's why you were so good," Mrs. Bradshaw said. "You knew each other. You hung out together after school."

"Being on the United will help Josh when he gets to high school," Mr. Bradshaw said. "If he keeps working hard, maybe he'll play in college."

Josh and his father shared a smile. Josh had always dreamed about playing soccer in college. His bedroom wall was plastered with posters and pennants from some of the best college soccer teams—Maryland, North Carolina, UCLA, and Indiana.

"How's Coach Hodges?" Mr. Bradshaw asked.

Josh sensed his father was trying to convince his mother that the United was a better team. "She's really good," he said. "She played four years at Notre Dame. She's much better than the Flames coach."

"Oh, I liked Mr. Daniel. He's a nice guy," his mother said as she reached out for the bag of chips again. Josh grabbed a few before handing it over.

"Will you guys stop eating!" Mr. Bradshaw said. "The chili's almost ready."

This time Josh traded smiles with his mother. Then he picked up the conversation again. "Mr. Daniel was a real nice guy. He just didn't know much about soccer. He's more of a baseball guy."

Mr. Bradshaw turned down the stove and looked at Josh. "Do you think Coach will start you at forward?"

Josh thought back on the five United practices. Coach seemed to be playing everyone an equal amount of time, as if she was still trying to find out who the best players were. Josh hoped he had shown Coach Hodges he was good enough to start. It would be so cool to tell the kids at school—especially his old Flames teammates—that he was starting for the United. "I don't know," he said. "Maybe. I think I'll get plenty of playing time, but I don't know about starting."

"How about Aidan?" his mother asked. "How's he doing?"

"About the same as me. I think he'll play a lot on defense."

"At least you guys didn't get cut," Mr. Bradshaw said.

"Did she really cut two kids?" Josh's mother asked, shaking her head.

"Yeah, really, Mom. You don't understand. This is serious soccer."

"Mr. Daniel would never have cut anyone." She pulled her phone out of her pocket and started checking her e-mails.

"Coach Hodges isn't a parent," Josh explained. "She's a real coach."

"You better get out of your sweaty soccer

stuff and wash up," Josh's father said. "We're going to eat soon. Two-minute warning." He looked over at his wife. "Any life-changing messages?" he asked with a smile.

"There's an e-mail from Coach Hodges."

"What's it say?" Josh asked. Changing his clothes could wait.

Josh's mother looked at the screen. "It looks like you have a tournament this weekend, Saturday and Sunday."

"Awesome! Coach said we were going to be in a couple tournaments before the season started."

"All right!" his father said, grabbing a fistful of air. "The United are going to take the pitch."

"It's in Johnstown," Mrs. Bradshaw said.

"Cool!" Josh exclaimed.

"Johnstown?" Mr. Bradshaw's arm fell to his side. "But that's a hundred miles away."

"Actually, it's 127 miles. I just checked," she said coolly. "The team will be playing at Johnstown Soccerplex. Coach Hodges booked rooms at a nearby hotel."

"Really?"

Mrs. Bradshaw handed her phone to Mr. Bradshaw.

"It looks like the tournament will take up the whole weekend," he said.

"We're in a real tournament!" Josh exclaimed. "I can't wait to text Aidan."

Mrs. Bradshaw turned to her husband and smiled. "I'm sure you and the United will have a good time in Johnstown this weekend."

Chapter 4

Oh, say does that star-spangled banner yet waaa-aaave...o'er the land of the freeeeeee...and the home of the...

Happy cheers drowned out the last word of the anthem. Eight teams in shiny uniforms stood proudly on the perfectly lined, sun-drenched field. Josh was standing with the United and couldn't believe he was part of all this excitement. It was never like this with the Flames.

The voice on the public address system boomed: "Let the twenty-fourth Annual Johnstown Labor Day Soccer Invitational begin!"

Some of the teams left with their fans to play on other fields. The United's first game was there in the main stadium. They were about to face the Phantoms.

"Come on, United!" Coach Hodges called. "Let's huddle up."

This is going to be great, Josh thought. He looked around the huddle and once again tried to match the faces with names. "What's the name of the big guy who plays defense?" Josh whispered to Aidan.

"Demetrius."

Coach Hodges began calling out the names of the starting lineup. "Aidan and Demetrius on the back line. Evan, you're at center midfield."

Josh leaned into the circle, hoping to hear his name.

"At forwards, Josh and Victor."

Josh and Aidan traded a quick nod. Yes! They were starting for the United!

Now I'm going to show them—Evan, Victor, everybody—that I'm as good as they are, Josh thought.

"Hands in," Coach Hodges ordered. The

team crowded closer and piled their hands on top of each other. "The Phantoms are good," Coach warned. "We're going to have to play hard and play smart. Hustle on three. "One...two...three..."

"Hustle!" the players shouted together.

The United hustled but it didn't help. Their passes were a little off, their offensive attack a step too slow. Evan threaded a pass to Josh as he rushed to the Phantoms goal, but the ball bounced off Josh's heel and he lost control. After that, Evan just passed to his buddy Victor, the other United forward— even when Josh was open.

Later, the United backline fell apart. Both Aidan and Demetrius moved to cover the same player. That left a Phantom forward wide open. In an instant, his team got him the ball and he blasted it into the United net.

Goal! The United was behind 1–0.

"C'mon, guys," Evan barked. "Don't bunch up. Play your position."

Aidan and Demetrius glared at each other.

"That was your guy!" Demetrius shouted.

"I thought you had him!" Aidan shouted back.

"Come on, guys, forget it," Josh said, clapping his hands. "Let's get it back."

The United couldn't get it back. They spent the rest of the game chasing the ball and trying to get their offense in gear. The Phantoms added another goal late in the second half to finish the scoring...and the United.

The United lost, 2–0.

Coach Hodges didn't say much after the game. She just shook her head. "You guys play like you've never seen each other before. This is a *team* sport. You better start getting your act together or get used to losing!"

Josh knew Coach Hodges was right, but that didn't make it easy to hear.

The players quickly gathered their stuff and went to check the large board showing the scores of the first games. Josh got there first.

"Who do we play in the second round?" Aidan asked.

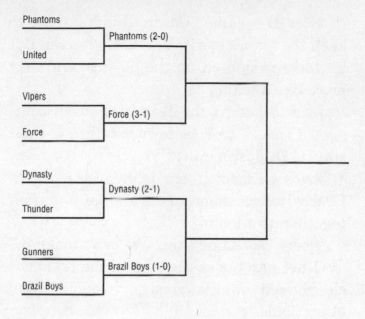

Phantoms

Phantoms (2-0)

United

Vipers

Force (3-1)

Force

Dynasty

Dynasty (2-1)

Thunder

Gunners

Brazil Boys (1-0)

Brazil Boys

"The Vipers," Josh answered. "We're in the losers bracket."

"Maybe they'll be easier to beat."

"I guess we'll find out."

But the second game was almost an exact replay of the first. The United players weren't clicking. There was no teamwork. No passing. No communication.

The United lost 2–0. Again.

After the game, Coach Hodges tried to keep the team's spirits up. "Good hustle. But we have to tighten up the defense and play more like a team."

Josh looked at the team's tired, discouraged faces. The coach wasn't lifting their spirits. Or Josh's either.

"Let's all meet in the lobby of the hotel," Coach Hodges suggested, "and go to dinner together as a team."

"Sorry," someone said. "We can't make it."

Other parents at the edge of the team circle chimed in. Everybody, it seemed, had other plans.

"We have some friends in the area. We're going to eat with them."

"What time is the game tomorrow?"

Coach Hodges threw up her hands. "All right, then. Everybody is on his own for dinner tonight," she said. "Just make sure you're in bed by ten o'clock. We have an early game tomorrow."

The United players and parents scattered. Josh and Aidan walked together toward Josh's father.

"Who are we playing tomorrow?" Aidan asked.

"I think we play the Thunder," Josh said.

"Are they any good?"

"Probably not," Josh said. "They're in the super-losers bracket—just like us."

Chapter 5

"Y ou look tired," Josh said to Aidan. The two boys were sitting in the hotel's breakfast room, eating cereal.

"I didn't sleep great last night," Aidan admitted.

"Why not?"

"It was so noisy. I don't know how you slept through it," Aidan said. "The bell on the elevator door kept going off. And somebody was getting ice from the ice machine every ten minutes. He must have been building an igloo in his room or something."

The boys laughed. Mr. Bradshaw sat down with his plate piled high. "Nothing I like better than a big country breakfast," he declared. "You boys ready to play?"

"Yeah."

"I guess so."

Mr. Bradshaw looked around the breakfast room. "Where's the rest of the team?" he asked. "I've hardly seen anyone."

Josh shrugged. "I don't know. We're pretty early. I guess we'll see them at the field."

The soccer pitch was quiet as the teams warmed up in the early morning chill. The dew was still on the grass, sparkling in the sunlight. The players' parents sat scattered in the stands, sipping coffee from thermoses.

"All right, let's play hard!" Coach Hodges shouted, clapping her hands together. "Same starting lineup as yesterday. Hustle on three."

Josh noticed that the team huddle was not as tight as the day before. And the shout of "One...two...three...hustle!" wasn't as loud.

Josh and Aidan walked onto the pitch, side by side. "It looks like you're not the only guy who had trouble sleeping last night," Josh said.

Sure enough, both teams were sluggish.

The action stayed stuck in the middle, with neither team managing a single shot on goal.

Late in the first half, Evan intercepted a crossing pass and dribbled upfield. When two Thunder players charged him, he tried to slip a quick pass to Josh. But the ball hit Josh's foot at a bad angle and sailed out of bounds.

"Oh, no!" Josh shouted.

The goalkeeper boomed a long punt back toward the United goal. Josh ran back to get in the action. *Man, nothing is working today,* he thought.

The score was tied 0–0 at halftime. The sun was rising and the morning warming. People kept coming in, filling up the stands. Many of them had come early to watch the next game.

The bigger crowd seemed to wake up the Thunder. They pounced on a turnover at midfield and sailed a crossing pass by the confused United defense. An alert Thunder forward knocked it in.

Goal! The United trailed, 1–0.

A few minutes later, the Thunder out-hustled the United for another goal. The United was behind 2–0. Again.

Coach Hodges put in some reserves.

Josh and Aidan stood on the sidelines with their arms folded across their chests. "Looks like we're going to lose another one," Aidan said.

"I don't know why." Josh dug his right cleat into the dirt. "We've got a lot of good players. Patrick West is a terrific goalkeeper. Victor is super fast and Mario can handle the ball." Josh lowered his voice. "I don't like Evan, but he can really play."

"Maybe we should all start wearing red shoes," Aidan said.

Josh didn't laugh. "We definitely need to do something."

Just then Coach Hodges called out, "Josh, Aidan, go in for Dylan and Thomas."

Josh raced back onto the pitch, eager to do something—anything—to get the United going.

Right away, Aidan, playing right fullback, stole the ball. He smartly dribbled away from the United goal and spotted Josh on the right wing. Instantly, the two old friends sensed the same play.

Josh spun and sprinted upfield. Aidan blasted a long pass up the right side. The Thunder scrambled after it, but Josh used his speed to outrun the defense and get the ball.

The Thunder goalkeeper jumped out to cut down Josh's angle to the goal. As Josh dribbled closer, he could sense the keeper hanging back, waiting for Josh to send a centering pass across the middle.

Josh knew that a centering pass to Evan or Victor was the correct play, but with the Thunder closing in, he decided to take a chance. *It's worth a try*, he thought.

He tapped the ball with his left foot, then blasted it with his right. The ball sizzled by the surprised goalkeeper, grazing the post before skipping into net.

Goal! The score was 2–1. Josh jumped up with a high fist-punch. His teammates swarmed him.

"Way to go, Josh!"

"We needed that!

"We're on a roll now!"

But the United were not on a roll.

The Thunder tightened their defense. There were no more goals. Not even any more shots on goal.

The United lost 2–1.

"We looked a little better this game. Way to go!" Coach Hodges shouted as the United players gathered their equipment and water bottles and the parents came down from the stands. "Remember, practice on Tuesday. We've got a lot to work on. Good goal, Josh. I'll e-mail everyone the information about next week's tournament."

"Where is it?"

"Perryville."

"Perryville?" Josh's father muttered. "That's even farther away."

In no time the team had disappeared into the parking lot and behind slamming car doors. Josh and Aidan lingered on the edge of the field. The sun was overhead and felt warm on Josh's back. The second game of the day was about to begin.

"Do you guys want to watch some of the next game?" Josh's dad asked.

Josh looked across the field, remembered the three United games—the three losses—and said, "No, let's get out of here. Maybe we'll do better next week."

Chapter 6

The second tournament was like the first—only worse. The United lost three games, playing once again in the losers bracket and then the super-losers bracket.

Josh had a goal in the second game but it wasn't enough. The team couldn't come together. It seemed that each United player was trying to score all by himself.

"We'll get better," Josh said to Aidan the next Monday at school. "We've got to. We can't get worse."

"Yeah. No wins. Six losses. That's bad," Aidan agreed as the two walked into the school cafeteria for lunch.

Josh could smell the food and see the steam rising from the silver heating trays. He grabbed a plate from a tall stack and moved down the cafeteria line. Aidan was right behind him.

"Man, I'm hungry," Aidan said. "What are we having today, spaghetti?"

"Nope. Sloppy joes," Josh announced.

Aidan made a face. "Maybe I'm not that hungry."

When they had their food, Josh looked for a place to sit. "Hey, look," he said, lifting his chin to point to a table across the room. "There's Chris and Nick from the Flames. Let's sit with them."

Josh slipped through the sea of middle schoolers, balancing his tray with one hand above his head like a waiter in a fancy restaurant. His old Flames teammates were busy eating, talking, and laughing.

"Got some room for us?" Josh asked as he swung his leg over the bench and squished in.

"Hey, watch it," Chris warned. "You're gonna knock my sloppy joe off the table."

"So what," Nick teased. "You'd still eat it."

"That's gross."

"Five-second rule," Nick said.

"What's that?" Josh asked.

"Don't you know anything?" Nick asked. "You can eat something that falls on the floor as long as you pick it up in less than five seconds."

"Maybe for something like potato chips," Josh said. "Not a sloppy joe."

"Well, now that depends," Aidan said. "If it falls on the bun, you're cool. But let's say the bun slips and sloppy joe stuff hits the floor. No way I'm eating it!"

"Especially off *this* floor," Josh added.

Chris held up his hands. "Could you guys change the subject? I'm losing my appetite." He took a bite and then eyed Josh. "How'd you guys do in that tournament this weekend?"

"They lost three games: 3–1, 2–1, and 2–0," Nick said before Josh could answer.

"How'd you know?" Aidan asked.

"I went on the United website," Nick said. "I always check on you guys. Looks like you're losing, big time."

Josh could feel his face burning. He bit

into his sloppy joe and secretly wished the United didn't have a website.

"Have the Flames started their season yet?" Aidan asked.

"Yeah, we played our first game on Saturday."

"How'd you do?" Aidan asked.

"We beat the Rampage, 3–1," Nick said. "You should've seen it. I set up Chris for the sweetest goal." Nick grabbed a couple of ketchup packages to demonstrate. "Chris passed it to me on the wing and I passed it right back to him in front of the goal. A perfect give and go."

Chris laughed. "Even I couldn't miss that one!" The two Flames traded high fives, and for a second Josh wondered if he should have stuck with his old team.

"So what gives with the United?" Nick asked. "I thought you guys would be great this season. That kid Evan Perry is supposed to be terrific. You got Kadir and Mario." He put his arm around Josh. "And the two best players from the Flames. Your team is loaded."

Aidan shrugged. "I don't know. We got a lot of guys who can play. We just don't play very well together."

Nick laughed. "If you two want to come back to the Flames, we might take you back." He took a bite of his sandwich. "By the way, Mr. Daniel says hi."

Josh kept his mouth closed and ate in silence. He was relieved when his friends stopped talking about the United and started arguing about whether LeBron James would be a good soccer player.

"LeBron's too tall to play soccer."

"Yeah, but he'd be great at heading the ball."

"And he'd be an awesome goalkeeper," Aidan declared. "He might even help our team."

Finally, Josh pushed away from the table. "These sloppy joes taste like they really did fall on the floor," he said as he swung his leg over the bench.

"Where are you going?" Aidan asked.

"I don't know," Josh said. "I just gotta get out of here."

Josh felt better as soon as he left the cafeteria. It was good to get away from the guys and all the talk about the United losing. Playing for the United was not nearly as much fun as Josh had thought it would be.

He headed straight for the media center and pulled up the United's record on one of the computers.

SCHEDULE & RESULTS

September 1	Labor Day Tournament	
	Phantoms	L 2-0
	Vipers	L 2-0
September 2	Thunder	L 2-1
September 8	Perryville Invitational	
	Extreme	L 3-1
	Real Team	L 2-1
September 9	Dynamo	L 2-0
September 15	Kings*	2 P.M.
September 22	Magic*	Noon
September 29	Storm*	10 A.M.
October 6	Red Devils*	Noon
October 13	Dynasty*	2 P.M.
October 20	Columbus Day Tournament	TBA
October 27	Future*	10 A.M.
November 3	Galaxy*	10 A.M.
November 10	Veterans Day Tournament	TBA
November 17	Majestics*	Noon
November 24	Arsenal*	2 P.M.
December 1	League Tournament	TBA
December 2	League Tournament	TBA

* League Games—All League Games will be played at the Soccerplex

His eyes settled on the United's first league game next Saturday.

We better beat the Kings, Josh thought. *Or maybe I will to go back to the Flames.*

Chapter 7

Josh raced down the pitch. "Evan!" he shouted, calling for the ball. "Lay it off!"

Evan ignored Josh and kept dribbling upfield. The Kings defense closed in on the United midfielder. Evan tried to squeeze between two defenders, but he stumbled and lost possession.

Josh stopped in his tracks. "Come on, Evan!" he shouted. "Pass the ball!"

But there was no time to waste arguing. The Kings were on the attack. Josh turned and ran back downfield, still thinking angry thoughts with every step. *I must've run up and down this field a hundred times and I've barely touched the ball. Maybe I should just join the track team.* He glanced at the score-board.

The score hadn't changed. The United still trailed, 1–0.

The Kings kept up the attack, passing quickly after one or two touches. The crisp passing kept the United defenders off balance, constantly chasing the ball.

A Kings wing slipped a dangerous pass toward the middle. A Kings forward bolted into the penalty area looking for a shot.

Desperate and a step behind, Aidan tried to get his foot on the ball. But his leg caught the guy's ankle and the two players tumbled in a heap 15 yards from the United goal.

Tweeeeeet! The referee blew his whistle, raced over, and stood above the two players. Pointing at Aidan, he pulled a yellow card from his shirt pocket and held it in the air. Penalty on Aidan. And a penalty kick for the Kings.

Aidan rolled over and pounded a fist into the ground. Several United players turned away with pained expressions clouding their faces and began to arrange themselves behind the Kings penalty kicker. Aidan joined them, his shoulders slumping and head down.

"Don't worry," Josh said. "You just got beat. It happens."

"Yeah, don't worry," Evan said, echoing Josh.

Surprised, Josh and Aidan turned toward their teammate.

"Don't worry," Evan repeated with a smirk. "Coach is going to have your butt on the bench so fast you won't have time to worry."

"Maybe," Aidan snapped, "if the midfielders came back every once in a while to help on defense instead of looking to score all the time—"

"Hey, if you can't keep up," Evan said, "go

back to rec league. You'll be a big star there."

"Shut up, both of you," Josh said, leaning forward. "Get ready for the rebound."

"There's not going to be one," Evan said, standing flat-footed in his red soccer shoes.

"How do you know?"

Evan pointed at the Kings player getting ready for the kick. "Do you know who that kid is?"

"No."

"Jason Jones."

"So?"

"So he's played on the regional teams," Evan explained. "Believe me, he's not gonna miss."

Sure enough, Jason Jones roofed a kick, high and hard, into the center of the net. Patrick, the United goalkeeper, didn't have a chance.

Goal! The United was behind 2–0. Again.

Evan was right about something else too. Coach put in a sub for Aidan, who jogged off the field, plopped on the bench, and buried his head in a towel.

The United still trailed 2–0 at halftime.

Coach Hodges was unusually quiet. Her lips were pressed together and her arms were folded tight across her chest as she watched the players gather around her, gulping water and chatting with each other.

When she spotted a couple of the boys standing off to the side, talking to their parents, she exploded. "Patrick! Kadir! Get over here. Now!"

The players huddled closer and gave Coach Hodges their full attention. She took a deep breath and began to talk. "Only one team in this game is playing like a team," she said, holding up a single finger. She pointed down the touchline to the Kings. "They are."

Josh could almost see the steam coming out of her ears. "I want quicker passes," she continued. "One, two touches. That's all. Then get the ball to somebody else."

"Evan!" Coach barked. Evan looked up, surprised. "The center midfielder is supposed to distribute the ball, not dominate it. Stop dribbling. Give the ball up. You've got to trust your teammates."

A small, secret smile swept across Josh's face. *Maybe now Mr. Red Shoes will pass me the ball.*

Coach Hodges wiped the smile off Josh's face by shouting *his* name. "Josh! Come back and help the midfielders. Don't just stand around waiting for the ball."

She paused and then said, "Now let's play more like a team in the second half!"

Coach's pep talk fired up the United for a while. Everyone—especially Evan—passed the ball better and created more chances in the second half. On one play, Evan laid off a quick touch to Josh, who blistered the ball toward the near post. But the Kings keeper dove and fisted the shot away.

Nursing a two-goal lead, the Kings played it safe. They dropped back their midfielders to help on defense. On offense, they played possession as much as they could. Time ticked away and the score never changed. Another 2–0 loss for the United.

After the game, Coach was more upbeat. "We played better in the second half," she declared. "More like a team. I liked the passing. We'll work on that more at next practice. See you Tuesday."

Josh and Aidan walked slowly away from the pitch.

"At least we played better in the second half," Josh said.

"What do you mean *we*?" Aidan said. "Coach parked me on the bench, remember?"

"Don't worry. You'll get more chances."

"I don't know. Coach isn't afraid of cutting people. Maybe she'll decide to cut me."

"She wouldn't cut anybody now. Not after the season has started."

"I'm not so sure about that," Aidan said. "Coach can be tough. We've lost seven games in a row. She's gonna want to do something to shake things up."

Josh swung his equipment bag over his shoulder. He walked toward his parents, who were waiting in the parking lot.

Aidan is right, he thought. *Something is going to have to change. And soon!*

Chapter 8

The bell sounded and two-dozen binders slammed shut. The students hurried toward the door. Ms. Littlewood, the social studies teacher, shouted above the noise, "Remember, get started on your projects this week. Don't leave all your research to the last minute."

"Ms. Littlewood," Josh said as he passed her desk. "Is it okay for Aidan and me to do our research project on the World Cup? I know we can find a lot of cool stuff about the soccer tournament and its history."

Ms. Littlewood looked up at Josh. She was shorter than some of her eighth grade students, but there was no doubt she was in charge. "I think the World Cup could be a great subject for your project," she said. "But don't just talk about who won or lost. I'd want to know how the tournament started— how it got to be such a big, worldwide event. And include something about the politics. Did you know they didn't have a World Cup in 1942 and 1946?"

"Why not?"

"World War II."

Josh started toward the door again. The project was sounding harder every time Ms. Littlewood opened her mouth.

"And don't leave out the women's tournaments," Ms. Littlewood said. Josh could almost see the ideas popping out of her head. "You could write about the 1999 United States women's team."

"Were they any good?"

"They won it all," Ms. Littlewood said, sounding a bit surprised at Josh's question. "Oh, right. You're too young to remember. They were a terrific team and I was a huge fan. If you have a couple of minutes, I'll tell you what I know about them. Not all of it will fit with your project, but it's a very interesting story."

Josh figured he didn't have a choice. And he sure didn't want to make his teacher mad at him. Plus, there was no soccer practice today.

Josh was very glad he stayed. While he listened to Ms. Littlewood talk about the 1999 women's team, an idea started forming in his head. As soon as he stepped out of the classroom, he texted Aidan.

Meet me @ my house. I will b there in 20.

"What's up?" Aidan asked as Josh opened the front door.

"I got a great idea!"

"For what?"

"For the United!" Josh said. "You won't believe it!" He dashed up the stairs. Aidan followed him.

"Keep it down!" Mr. Bradshaw shouted from his office. "I'm trying to work."

Josh flopped down on his unmade bed.

Aidan sat backward on the desk chair and grabbed a mini football from the cluttered desk. "So what's the great idea?" he asked, tossing the ball to Josh.

Josh flipped it back to him. "Okay, so I was talking to Ms. Littlewood after school about doing our research project on the World Cup—"

"What did she say?" Aidan lobbed the ball back to Josh.

"She's cool with it. But that's not what I want to tell you."

"So what do you want to tell me?"

"I'm trying to get to it!" Josh threw the ball hard at his buddy.

"Ouch!" Aidan laughed. "Take it easy."

"Listen. This is serious," Josh said. "So Ms. Littlewood starts telling me all about the 1999 United States Women's World Cup team. They were kind of like the United—"

"Are you saying we're like a girls' team?"

"Aidan, will you shut up! They were a totally great team. Ms. Littlewood knew all about them," Josh said, the words tumbling out. "They beat China in the World Cup final on penalty kicks in front of 90,000 people at the Rose Bowl. They had Mia Hamm, this fantastic forward, who scored more international goals than anybody. Even the guys. They also had Kristine Lilly, who played in more international matches than anybody. Something like 350!"

"Really?" Aidan seemed impressed.

"Yeah, and their midfielder Michelle Akers was a great player, a complete monster," Josh continued. "They were a huge deal. The whole country loved them. The team was on late night shows, TV ads, and magazine covers. They were even *Sports Illustrated* Sportswomen of the Year."

"The whole team?"

Josh nodded. "The whole team."

"So what's your big idea?" Aidan asked. "Are you going to get Mia Hamm and Michelle what's-her-name to play for the United?"

Josh laughed. "They would help." Then he turned serious again. "Ms. Littlewood said the 1999 team used to do team-building exercises."

"What are those?"

"They're special activities—they don't

even have to be soccer stuff. They're like weird kinds of games or puzzles that the team has to work on together. They help the players become more of a team. Ms. Littlewood said the 1999 team even had a coach for team building."

"So where are you going with this?" Aidan asked.

"Don't you get it? The United should do team-building exercises," Josh declared. "Just like the 1999 team. I mean, the United are a bunch of All-Stars—"

"Yeah, and we're still losing," Aidan interrupted again.

"That's my point," Josh said. "We're All-Stars from different teams—just like the 1999 team. We need to do something to become more of a real team."

"Like the Flames used to be?"

"Yeah, just like the Flames," Josh said, thinking back to all his years on the old team. "But the Flames were together so long, it was easy for them to be a team. The United have to do something more."

"Okay, now what?"

"Okay, now we have to find some team-building exercises." Josh pulled his laptop out from under a jacket on his bed and logged on. "Let's see if we can find a website or something." He typed the keywords into the search bar.

"Look. There's a ton of stuff!" Josh turned the laptop so Aidan could see. Then he clicked on one of the sites. A list of team-building games and activities appeared on the screen.

"Yeah, but what are you gonna do?" Aidan asked. "Tell Coach how to run her practices?"

Josh grabbed the mini football again and rolled it around in his hands. "I don't know. I definitely don't want to talk to her in front of the whole team."

Aidan nodded. "Yeah, Evan and Victor would probably think it was a stupid idea, especially if it came from you and me."

The boys threw the ball back and forth, thinking. Finally, Aidan asked, "So how are we going to get coach to do this?"

"We could e-mail her with our *suggestion*," Josh said.

"Sure, she's always e-mailing us stuff about the team."

Josh picked up his laptop. "Get out of the chair," he ordered Aidan.

"Why?"

"We got to write something." Josh slid off the bed and sat in the chair. He pushed aside some papers and a dirty sock from the desk and put down the laptop. Aidan stood behind him.

"We'll say it's from both of us, okay?" Josh said, glancing over his shoulder at Aidan.

"Yeah. Tell her we're working on a school project."

For the next ten minutes the boys worked together on the message to their coach. When they finished, they looked over what they had written.

From: Joshua@Bradshaw333family.com
To: ilovesoccer@coachhodges.com
Subject: Idea for the United

Coach Hodges,

Aidan and I are working on a research project for school on the World Cup. Our teacher told us about the US women's team that won the World Cup in 1999. She said they used special team-building exercises to become a better team.

We are thinking we should try some of those team-building exercises on the United. It might be worth a try. After all, most of the guys on the team haven't played together before this season and we're not doing very well (0–7) so far.

It's just an idea. We're not telling you how to coach the team or anything. We thought it might help. We hope everything is okay with you.

Josh Bradshaw
Aidan McFarland

Aidan pointed at the screen. "Maybe we should attach one of those websites you found. You know, a site with a list of team-building exercises."

"Good idea." Josh tapped some keys and then looked at Aidan. "Should we send it?"

"Why not? Aidan said. "What have we got to lose? The worst thing that can happen is she'll ignore it."

"No," Josh said. "The worst thing that can happen is that she tries it, and it doesn't work. Then what?" Josh took a deep breath and hit the send button.

Aidan sat on the bed and the boys went back to tossing the football around. "Who we playing next?"

"The Magic."

"Are they any—"

Josh's computer made a clicking sound. "Hey, I've got mail," he said. "I wonder if it's from the coach." Josh pulled up the e-mail and read the message aloud.

From: ilovesoccer@coachhodges.com
To: Joshua@Bradshaw333family.com
Subject: RE: Idea for the United

Josh & Aidan—

Thanks for your e-mail. I'm glad you're thinking about the team. I know all about the 1999 Women's World Cup team. They were my idols when I was growing up. Let's talk on Tuesday about what we can do. I'll meet you two guys at the pitch twenty minutes before practice.

See you Tuesday.
Coach Hodges

Chapter 9

J osh and Aidan stretched a huge purple blanket out on the grass next to the United's practice field.

Coach Hodges walked up behind the boys with her brown equipment bag over her shoulder. "Hey guys. What's up? Are we having a picnic today?" she joked.

Aidan looked at Josh. "It's your idea," he said. "Go ahead, tell her."

"Okay." Josh took a deep breath. "Remember what we said in our e-mail about the 1999 Women's World Cup team using team-building exercises to get better?"

"I remember," Coach said. "That team did a whole bunch of strange stuff. It must have worked; they were awesome."

"Yeah. I figured we should try something like that," Josh said. "We got a lot of good players—Evan, Victor, Demetrius, me, and Aidan. We just don't play like a team."

"We gotta do something," Aidan added. "We're 0–7."

"I hear you," Coach Hodges said. "So what's with the purple blanket?"

"It's an old one," Josh said. "We use it for picnics. Purple's my mom's favorite color."

"No, Josh. I mean how are you going to use it for team building?"

"Oh, right," Josh said. "I got the idea from a website. Here's how it goes: We all get on the blanket—all eighteen of us. We pretend it's like a boat stranded in a river swarming with alligators and we have to get to shore."

"Okay. Where's the shore?" Coach asked.

Josh motioned to Aidan. "Give me your water bottle." Josh counted off twenty steps and placed his water bottle and Aidan's on the ground. "Let's say this is the shore."

"How are we gonna get the blanket all the way over there?" Aidan asked. "I mean, everybody will be standing on it."

"Did the website explain how to do it?" Coach Hodges asked.

"Not really," Josh said. He could feel his face turning red.

"That's good," Coach said. "Now all of you guys can figure it out together. That was the whole point of the exercises for the U.S. team—to practice working together." She looked down at the blanket and then up at Josh. "We'll try it today."

Suddenly Josh got nervous. What if his big idea—the team-building exercises—was a big flop? What if everybody thought it was a big joke? Why did he bring the *purple* blanket?

After the team arrived, the United practice went the way it always did—with lots of drills: Passing. Dribbling. Corner kicks. Trapping. Defense. Crossing passes and heading.

Coach Hodges never mentioned the blanket. Josh had almost forgotten about it by the time Coach blew her whistle, ninety minutes into the two-hour practice. "Follow me," she said. "We're going to try something different." She gathered the players around the blanket. "Josh, why don't you explain this setup?"

Josh swallowed hard. He thought Coach Hodges would explain the team-building exercise. Josh could feel the eyes of his teammates on him. He felt like he was on the spot, like someone taking a penalty kick.

"This is a...um...team-building exercise," Josh started. "Like the 1999 United States women's team used to do."

"Who?" Evan asked.

"The 1999 United States Women's World Cup team," Josh repeated. "They had great players—a lot of them—but they weren't playing well together so they tried some team-building exercises."

"What happened?" Victor asked.

"I know," said Mario. "They won the World Cup!"

"Let's give Josh a chance to explain," Coach said, nodding for him to continue.

Josh told everyone a little more about the 1999 team and what they did to become better teammates.

"Me and Aidan—and Coach—figured maybe some team-building exercises would help us play better too." He paused for a moment, then continued. "I mean we got a lot of real good players...and, um—"

"Josh, why don't you tell everyone about the exercise you've set up over here," Coach suggested.

"Okay," Josh said. "See, this blanket is like a boat surrounded by hungry alligators and we're all on the boat and we need to get it to shore."

"Where's the shore?" Victor asked.

Josh pointed. "Where Aidan and I put our water bottles."

"Why don't we just lift it up and move it there?" Patrick asked.

"You can't get off the boat or you'll be alligator food," Aidan said, raising one hand high and slamming it down on the other like the jaws of an alligator.

Everyone on the team laughed, except Evan. "Come on, Coach. What's this got to do with soccer?"

Coach Hodges fixed the center midfielder

in a level gaze. Josh had never seen his coach look like this before. She answered Evan with one word: "Everything." Then the coach set her watch and walked toward a shady tree. "You have twenty minutes," she said. "Or you're all going to be alligator food."

Nobody spoke at first. They all crowded onto the blanket.

"This is stupid," Evan muttered.

"Come on," Demetrius said. "Let's give it a try."

Evan stared at Josh. "It's your brilliant idea. How do we do it?"

"I don't know. We got to figure that out as a team," Josh said. "That's the whole point."

"Who made you coach?" Evan demanded. "Why do *we* have to do this...just because of some girls' team?"

"That girls' team won the World Cup," Josh snapped.

"So what," Evan barked.

"So that sounds a lot better than 0–7," Victor said softly.

Evan didn't have an answer for that.

"I got an idea," Mario said, puzzling out the problem. "Maybe we can all shuffle our feet and kind of scoot the blanket to shore."

"Let's try it," Kadir said.

"Okay," Mario said. "Everyone face the shore. Ready? One...two...three...shuffle."

"That makes it sound like we're dancing!" Evan complained.

"Just shuffle, Evan!" everyone yelled.

The team shuffled forward, but the blanket just got twisted up in their feet.

"Hey, watch out!" Kadir shouted. "This is making the boat smaller."

"Whoa!" Patrick yelled as he fell off the blanket. "You guys are going to need a new goalie. I think an alligator just ate my foot."

Victor hopped up. "Wait! I got an idea!" Everyone stopped laughing and listened. "Maybe we can each grab the edge and jump forward."

When the players were all in position, Victor shouted, "One...two...three—jump!"

They jumped, but yanking on the blanket made them lose their balance. Most of the players tumbled off. Everyone was laughing now, even Evan. "Hey! The alligators ate half our team!"

"Fifteen minutes," Coach Hodges called from the shade.

"C'mon, guys. Let's start over," Josh said. "I got an idea. Everybody get to the front of the boat."

The boys crammed onto the front of the blanket. "Hey, quit pushing," Victor protested. "I don't want to end up with the alligators again."

"Here's my idea," Josh told the players. "You know how an inchworm moves? First it's flat. Then it pulls up in the middle. Then it stretches forward and it's flat again."

"Yeah. That's how they move. They keep doing that," Patrick said. "We used to race them at summer camp."

"Right. Come on, Evan," he said, motioning with his hand. "I need you to help me. Everyone else stay where you are." Evan followed Josh to the middle of the blanket. "Okay, let's pull up here to make a bump like an inchworm." Josh and Evan pulled at the same time. The back of the blanket inched closer as they tugged the middle higher.

"Okay, now everybody step over the middle and go to the back of the boat," Josh called. The players stepped over the bump and squeezed onto the remaining strip of blanket. Josh continued giving orders. "Now, Evan, Victor, Aidan, and me will push the blanket forward."

The boys leaned over the bump in the middle and started pushing and heaving the front of the blanket toward the water bottles and the "shore." When the bump was flat and they had pushed as much as they could, the players eyed their progress.

"We only gained about a foot!" Kadir said.

"Ten minutes!" Coach Hodges called out.

"That's okay," Evan said. "If we keep it up, we'll make it. Everyone to the front again, so Josh and I can pull up the back."

Working together, all of the boys got into a rhythm. Move to the front. Pull up the middle. Step to the back. Push out the front. Move to the front. Pull up the middle. Step to the back....

They were in constant motion, bumping into each other and laughing about it. Mario almost fell off the boat, but Patrick yanked him back. The steady chatter kept everyone pumped and focused.

"Make the bump bigger. That'll make the boat go faster."

"Let's have more guys push the blanket flat."

"We should name our boat the U.S.S. *Inchworm.*"

When the front edge of the blanket reached the water bottle, they all cheered.

"We are the United!"

"We're not alligator food!

"Let's hear it for the U.S.S. *Inchworm!*"

Aidan started to laugh. "Hey, we finally got a win!"

Coach Hodges joined the celebration. "Good work, United," she said, smiling and checking her watch. "You made it with a minute to spare." She clapped her hands and added, "See you Thursday. And, Josh, I've got a research project for you."

Josh looked at his coach, wondering what she meant.

"Find me another team-building exercise," she said. "We'll do it after the next practice."

The players cheered. They kept laughing and talking about the U.S.S. *Inchworm* and the day's different kind of practice. Josh realized the United had laughed more today than they had during the whole first part of the season.

"See you later, alligators!" Aidan shouted as he walked away.

Even Evan smiled. "That wasn't too bad," he admitted. Then he looked at Josh and added, "But let's see how we do—as a team— on Saturday."

Tweeeeeet! The referee's whistle blew, ending the first half. Josh glanced at the scoreboard even though he knew the score of the game.

UNITED		MAGIC
0	0.00 HALF 1	2

The United was losing again, 2–0.

The players drank their water in silence. They sat near a corner of the pitch where the grass was still thick and green. Aidan leaned toward Josh and whispered, "Coach doesn't look very happy."

"I don't blame her," Josh said without looking up. "We stunk in the first half."

Coach Hodges stared down at her clipboard as if she was stalling for time, trying to control her temper. Finally she stepped forward and spoke to the team in a firm voice. "We'll start the second half with the same starting lineup." Her finger jabbed the air and her voice got louder. "But I am telling the starters right now, you have ten minutes—ten minutes—to make something happen. Or I'll find some other players who will."

She paced back and forth, then turned and barked out more instructions to the team. "One or two touches. Pass the ball. Don't dribble so much. Don't try to do it all yourself. Trust your teammates. Share the ball. Work together. We practiced being a team, now play like one." She flashed the fingers on her left hand twice. "Remember, you have ten minutes."

The United walked back onto the pitch. Their heads were still down. Evan glanced at Josh. "Looks like your team-building ideas aren't working."

Josh turned and looked right at him. "The exercises can't make you play like a team. *We* have to do that."

For the first few minutes of the second half, the United continued their sloppy play with the ball stuck around midfield. Out of the corner of his eye, Josh could see the United reserves jogging along the sidelines, warming up.

Coach Hodges wasn't kidding when she said ten minutes, Josh thought.

He got the ball on the wing and quickly sized up the situation. He was tempted to dribble the ball as far as he could, but remembered Coach's instructions. "Trust your teammates. Don't try to do it all yourself." So he angled the ball to Evan.

Josh had another thought: *I wonder if he'll ever pass it back to me.*

As if he could read Josh's mind, Evan slipped around a Magic defender and fired a pass back to Josh, who was racing up the wing.

Josh controlled the ball with a quick touch, then skidded a low, hard centering pass back to Evan, now in perfect scoring position. With one swift kick, Evan redirected the ball right into the net.

Goal! The score was 2–1. The United were back in the game.

"Perfect give and go!" Josh shouted as the team celebrated around Evan.

"Great centering pass!" Evan cheered, pointing at Josh.

As the players took their positions, Josh checked the stadium clock. *Nine minutes*, he thought. *Just in time!*

The United continued to control play in the second half with short, crisp passes. Just as Coach had instructed, one or two touches and the ball would be on its way to another United player. The new United attack created more scoring chances. Victor forced the keeper to make a great save. Josh boomed a shot that rattled off the crossbar. Evan blasted a shot that sailed just wide of the post.

Coach Hodges paced the sidelines, clapping her hands and shouting. "Way to go! Keep trying! Keep it moving! Go for the goal!"

The team kept getting chances and corner kicks, but still no goals. Time was winding down. The Magic threatened, pushing the ball deep into the United zone. But Aidan intercepted a pass and the United pressed the attack.

Everyone kept passing the ball to an open teammate. First to the wing, then to the middle and back to the wing, edging closer to the Magic goal and always keeping possession.

Josh slipped the ball inside to Evan, just outside the penalty area. Then Josh darted to an opening between two Magic defenders, hoping Evan would spot him.

He did!

Evan drilled a quick pass back to Josh, who slipped between the two defenders and broke into the clear. The Magic goalkeeper stepped out to challenge Josh. But with the slightest touch, Josh shifted the ball from one foot to the other, spun around the keeper, and fired a shot low and hard into the net.

Goal! The score was tied, 2–2.

A few minutes later the referee blew his whistle to end the game. The United team celebrated in the middle of the field, smiling and slapping backs as if they had won. The players were still celebrating while they gathered up their water bottles and equipment bags.

"Come on, it was just a tie," Aidan said. "You guys are acting like we won the World Cup."

But the United were not listening to any of that talk. "Are you kidding me? A tie feels great," Josh declared.

"Especially after seven straight losses," Evan added.

Coach Hodges was standing at the edge of the field with her equipment bag full of soccer balls slung over her shoulder. "Hey, Josh," she called as he walked by. "I was wondering. How's your research project coming? You know, the one you're doing for me?"

Josh smiled. "I've got a real interesting idea for the next exercise."

Chapter 11

Josh and Aidan stepped out of the car at the High-Top Adventure Park. The gravel parking lot was surrounded by woods. Through the just-turning leaves, Josh could see zip lines, swinging ropes, and wobbly bridges high in the trees. And he could hear the sound of distant laughter and happy yells.

Josh eyed Aidan. "I told Coach about this place. I wasn't sure she'd let us come."

"Yeah, I remember when we came here with the Flames last year," Aidan said. "It's cool."

"When will you guys be done?" Josh's mother asked, leaning out of the car window.

"In two hours. Like a regular practice."

"Okay, I'll pick you up then."

The two boys saw the rest of the United team gathered near a small cabin at the edge of the woods.

"Come on, guys," Coach Hodges called, waving them over. "Hustle over here."

Coach had a big grin on her face as she addressed the team. "Josh tells me this place is a lot of fun." She looked back at the trees. "The park has lots of different climbing elements and courses. I'm going to break you into small groups. After you get safety instructions from one of the park rangers, you can spend the rest of the time climbing. Remember, stay together and help each other out. Be good teammates."

She glanced at her clipboard and started calling out the climbing teams. "The first group will be Josh, Evan, and Kadir."

Josh's group walked over to a big ladder made of angled logs nailed to a board. It led up to a platform that looked like the world's coolest tree house.

Evan glanced around at the ropes and cables high in the trees. "This is a pretty weird soccer pitch."

"Don't worry, it's cool," Josh said. "I came here last year with my old team, the Flames. We—"

"Whoa! Look at that!" Evan's eyes widened and he pointed into the trees.

Josh turned toward a loud, metallic whirring sound. High above them, a girl with her harness attached to a zip line flew between two trees.

"Yeeeeaaaaahhhhh!" Her voice filled the air.

A park employee approached Josh's group. He was tall and wore a bright orange T-shirt with the words "High-Top Adventure Park— It's Tree-mendous!"

"Hi, I'm Berkeley," he smiled. "How are you guys doing today?" Berkeley eyed their United shirts. "Let me guess. Same soccer team?"

"Yeah."

"How're you doing this season?"

"Not so good," Josh admitted. "Our record's 0–7–1."

"But we played a lot better our last game," Evan added.

"Maybe this'll help you play even better," Berkeley said. For the next fifteen minutes he explained the park and its safety features while the boys stepped into their climbing harnesses, fastened the straps, and put on thick leather gloves.

"We use a double-clip system, so there's no way anyone can fall. It's totally safe. Stay away from the black-diamond and double-diamond courses. Those are for the expert climbers. Stick to the yellow, green, and blue courses. Those are easier. Remember, only one guy on an element at a time. And one more thing—have fun."

"Aren't you coming with us?" asked Kadir.

Berkeley shook his head. "No, I'll stay down here. But don't worry, somebody will climb up and help you if you get in trouble."

The boys scrambled up the log ladder and stood on the platform. A maze of cables, ropes, planks, beams, and barrels spread out into the trees like a midair obstacle course.

"Which way should we go?" Evan asked.

"Why don't we try the blue course?" Josh suggested, pointing the way.

The boys started off with Josh leading the way, Evan next, and Kadir going third. First they tried a hanging bridge made of strung-together wooden footboards. Josh gripped the taut wire railings and moved slowly, getting used to the height, taking one careful step at a time across the bridge. He tried not to look down. When he reached the other side, he let out a rush of air. "Come on, it's fun," he called back to his teammates.

Evan started, moving even more slowly than Josh across the hanging bridge. Kadir was the slowest. Standing on the platform waiting, Josh whispered to Evan, "He doesn't look like he likes it up here."

The boys proceeded through the other elements on the blue course: a rope pulled tight like a high wire in the circus, a bridge made of horizontal logs spaced really far apart, and a maze of boards hung at different heights and angles.

Best of all was the zip line, where Josh sailed through the air for about twenty yards, screaming all the way. When he reached the end, he yelled to Evan and

Kadir, still on the starting platform. "C'mon! It's great!"

Evan hesitated for a few seconds before pushing off, but as he flew fast and high toward Josh he was smiling from ear to ear.

Kadir waited forever on the platform. He seemed to be trying to summon up the courage to step off. Finally he closed his eyes, leaned forward, and stepped out into thin air, letting the zip line propel him through the trees.

Josh watched Kadir zoom toward him. As Kadir got close, Josh—still clipped to the safety cable—pulled him to the platform.

"Way to go!" Evan yelled.

The final element was the toughest. It was a bridge made with high "railings" and a series of long U-shaped cables strung between them. They looked like a bunch of big stirrups. When Josh grabbed the railing and stepped into the first big loop, everything—his feet, his hands, his whole body—swung wildly. He had to steady himself before he could step into the next big loop. His heart beat fast as he slowly edged from one shaky perch to another. When he finally made it to the other side, he hugged the tree. After he caught his breath, he turned back to Evan and Kadir. "Take your time," he warned them. "This one's tough. Make sure your foot's really in the loop."

Like Josh, Evan moved slowly, trembling on each loop. When he finally made it onto the platform, he gave Josh a high five and then the two of them turned to watch Kadir.

Kadir started across cautiously, almost painfully, stepping from loop to loop. When he got halfway across, he froze.

"Uh-oh," Josh breathed. He could see it in Kadir's eyes. "He's panicking," Josh whispered to Evan.

"Just take it one step at a time," Evan called. "Remember what Berkeley said. You're clipped on. You can't fall. You can do it."

Kadir reached out with his foot, but he started to shake again and lost his nerve.

Josh and Evan didn't give up on their teammate. They kept encouraging him.

"That's it."

"You can do it."

Slowly, carefully, Kadir started again. He stepped tentatively from loop to loop, edging closer to the platform. Then he froze again.

"You keep talking to him," Josh said. "I'll go get him."

"Wait. Only one guy on an element, remember?" Evan warned.

"Oh yeah," Josh said as he stepped back onto the platform. "But we've got to help him. We can't just leave him out there." He looked at Kadir. He hadn't moved. "Are you okay, Kadir?"

His teammate didn't answer.

Josh stepped back into the loops toward Kadir. "Don't worry, Kadir. We'll help you!" Josh shouted. "Go, United."

Josh reached out and got a firm grip on Kadir's hand. "I got you," he said. He slowly led his teammate across the final loops to the platform.

Kadir was still shaking as he stood on the solid wood platform. "Thanks," he said in a whisper.

"No problem," Josh said. Evan patted Kadir on the back.

"I must have looked pretty stupid out there, not moving," Kadir said, his voice coming back. "I won't be much help against the Storm on Saturday if I freeze like that."

"That's all right," Josh said. "I don't think we'll play the Storm up here in the trees."

The three teammates laughed and climbed together down to solid ground.

Chapter 12

"Ten...eleven...twelve..." A circle of players tapped the ball to each other in a pregame warm-up of "soccer tennis," working hard to keep the ball in the air. Their shouts filled the field.

"Don't let it drop!"

"Get it!"

"Good save!"

Josh looked around the small cluster of players as the count got higher.

"Thirteen...fourteen...fifteen..."

Victor...Kadir...Evan...Mario...Patrick... Demetrius.... Josh hadn't known these guys before the season. Now they were beginning to become real teammates.

Coach Hodges and Josh had found more

team-building exercises to end each practice. The team liked the exercises. In fact, some of the other players had made suggestions.

Victor had come up with "trust falls." He had the team break into pairs. One player had to close his eyes, fold his arms across his chest, and fall backward, trusting his team-mate to catch him.

It wasn't easy. The first time Josh fell back, he could feel his arms twitch and his legs shift to stop his fall. With his eyes shut, it was hard to believe Kadir would catch him.

"You have to trust your teammates to catch you," Coach Hodges had said. "And maybe if we learn to trust each other in prac-tice, we'll learn to trust each other during the game."

Still, Josh worried that the team-building exercises weren't enough. They were fun and seemed to be bringing the team together, but they hadn't led to a United win. Yet.

Josh was thinking about all that as the game of soccer tennis continued.

"Twenty…twenty-one…twenty-two…"

Then suddenly the ball popped a little too far. Josh reached for it but couldn't get it. The game was over.

"Twenty-two!" Patrick announced.

"That's our best ever!" Mario exclaimed.

Twenty-two is pretty good, Josh thought. *But it would be better if we won just one game. Today's game!*

The United played well in the first half but they were up against a tough team—the Storm—and the score stayed tied 0–0.

The United had missed some scoring chances. Late in the first half, Josh got free near the top of the penalty area and blistered a shot on goal, but it sailed just over the crossbar. When he turned away in disappointment, he saw Evan clapping and cheering him on, the way they had encouraged Kadir when he was stuck on the blue course. "Good shot!" the United midfielder shouted to Josh. "Keep taking those shots."

Josh's hopes for a win were high when the United raced back onto the pitch for the second half. Still, the score stayed knotted at

0–0 until midway through the second half.

The Storm put pressure on the United goal. Aidan made a strong play to run a Storm attacker off the ball and gain control. He passed the ball to Demetrius, another United defender, as the Storm fell back.

Patrick, the United goalkeeper, called for the ball. Demetrius, without looking, kicked the ball slowly back toward Patrick and the United goal.

Upfield, Josh got ready for a long punt, but as he saw the play develop, he screamed. "No!"

A quick-thinking Storm forward spun and got to the ball. In a flash, he tipped it past the frantic United keeper and angled it into the net.

Goal!

The Storm was ahead, 1–0.

Stunned, the United huddled in the middle of the field.

Aidan moaned. "I can't believe—"

But before he could finish, Evan cut him off. "Forget it," he said. "We'll be okay. Let's stick together and get it back."

"Fast," Josh added.

The United put pressure on the Storm goal right away. With quick passes and a series of give and gos, the United were buzzing around the Storm's net.

Evan faked left and dribbled right, bringing the Storm defense with him. Watching the play unfold, Josh circled left, hoping to get another shot near the top of the penalty area.

Seeing his teammate, Evan pivoted and laid a pass off for Josh. This time Josh did not miss. He hit the ball squarely and drilled a hard shot just inside the far post and past the diving Storm goalkeeper.

Goal! It was all tied, 1–1.

The United crowded around Josh to celebrate. But Josh and Evan wouldn't let them celebrate too much.

"We need another one."

"We still have time."

"Don't let up."

The United went right back on the attack.

Josh settled a pass on the wing. Seeing an opening to the goal, he rushed forward, attacking the net. The Storm defenders and keeper reacted quickly to cut him off, so Josh chipped a high, soft pass to an open space near the Storm goal.

Evan sprinted to the ball. After letting it take a single bounce, he volleyed it into the back of the net.

Goal! The United were ahead, 2–1.

This time the United celebrated in a wild, roiling circle. When the game ended a few minutes later, they celebrated all over again with chest bumps, high fives, and loud cheers.

The United had beaten the Storm, 2–1, for their first win of the season.

The players didn't want to leave the pitch after the victory. Even when they finally walked off together, they were still talking about the win.

"What a comeback!"

"Bring on Manchester United."

"We got a one-game winning streak!" Evan shouted as he pumped a finger to the sky.

"And a two-game undefeated streak!" Aidan added.

Josh elbowed Evan. "Watch out guys," he said. "Evan's gonna want to score all the time now."

"Don't worry about that," Evan said.

"Why not?" Josh asked. "After all, you got the game winner, didn't you?"

Evan smiled. "I was just helping the U.S.S. *Inchworm* get to shore."

W hat's for lunch?" Josh asked as he pushed his tray along the cafeteria line.

"Chicken nuggets and tater tots," Aidan answered.

Josh shrugged. "I guess that's better than sloppy joes." When he reached the end of the line, he looked around the cafeteria. "There's Chris and Nick. Let's go sit with them again."

Josh and Aidan made their way to a table in the far corner. "Hey, guys," Josh said. "Got any room for a couple of old teammates?"

"Sure."

Josh and Aidan sat down and started eating their lunch.

"I know why you guys are so cheery," Chris said. "You finally won one."

"Are you checking our website *every* week?" Aidan asked.

"Haven't missed a week yet," Chris replied.

This time Josh was glad the United had a website.

Chris elbowed Josh. "I saw you got another goal too. How many goals you got this year?"

"Four. Four in nine games," Josh said. "How'd the Flames do on Saturday?"

"We won again, 4–1," Nick said.

"We played great," Chris said. "We had the ball in their zone the whole game."

The boys ate in silence for a while. One of Josh's chicken nuggets slipped out of his hand onto the floor.

Chris started counting. "One second...two seconds..."

"No way I'm picking that up off the floor and eating it," Josh said.

"Come on," Chris insisted. "Five-second rule."

"Forget it."

Chris leaned back from the table. "So what's the big difference? Why did you guys finally win one?"

"I don't know," Aidan said. "We just played more like a team. You know, passing it around. Especially in the second half." He looked at Josh and added, "Then there was Josh's great idea."

"What was that?"

Josh popped a tater tot into his mouth. "I suggested to Coach Hodges a couple weeks ago that we do some kind of team-building exercise every practice."

"Like what?" Nick asked.

"One was with a blanket. We all stood on it and had to move it about 20 feet," Josh said.

"What's so hard about that? Chris asked.

"We were all standing on the blanket!" Aidan pointed out. "We weren't allowed to get off."

"Did you guys do it?" Nick asked.

"Yeah. It took us about twenty minutes, but we did it."

Chris looked puzzled. "What's that got to do with soccer?" he asked.

"Everything," Josh and Aidan said at the same time, then laughed.

"We even went to the High-Top Park like the Flames did after last season," Josh added. "Climbed on all those ladders and ropes and zip lines. It was fun."

"I still don't get what it has to do with soccer," Chris said.

Aidan broke in again before Josh could even open his mouth. "The 1999 United States women's team used this kind of team-building stuff," he said. "And they won the World Cup. They were *Sports Illustrated* Sportswomen of the Year."

"Since when are you the big expert?" Nick asked.

"We're doing our research paper for Ms. Littlewood on the World Cup," Josh explained. "Hey, don't knock it. These team-building exercises are working. We're playing great."

"You guys are talking pretty big for a team that's only won one game," Chris said.

"What?" Josh said. "You think the Flames could beat the United?"

"Yeah," Chris said. Then he smiled and held up a tater tot. "In a game of tater-tot toss."

"What's a tater toss tot...I mean—"

"Tater tot toss," Chris corrected. "You gotta toss a tater tot into your teammate's mouth from across the table. Let's say the best out of three tosses. Flames against the United."

"We gotta make sure Ms. Littlewood doesn't see us," Aidan said. "She's on lunch duty today."

"We're way back in the corner," Chris said. "She won't see a thing." He picked up a tater tot from his plate. "We'll go first. Come on, Nick, open up."

Nick opened his mouth. Chris held the tater tot like a dart, eyeing the distance across the lunchroom table. He let it go with a quick flick of his wrist. The greasy puff of potato flew across the table and bounced right off Nick's nose.

Everyone at the table laughed.

"Zero for one!" Aidan shouted.

"Come on, Nick, you gotta move your mouth," Chris said.

"All right, our turn," Josh said, holding up a tater tot. He closed one eye, trying to zero in on Aidan's lower jaw.

Josh's throw was perfect. The tater tot landed on Aidan's tongue and he snapped his mouth shut.

"Goal!" Josh shouted. "The United lead, 1–0."

Nick's next toss landed on Chris's forehead and then fell to the floor. Aidan missed Josh's head entirely, but the United team still led, 1–0.

"Okay, last try," Chris said. "The pressure's on." Chris's toss sailed true and the tot zoomed right into Nick's wide-open mouth.

"Goal!" Chris shouted. "Tie score."

"Keep it down," Aidan warned. "Ms. Littlewood is looking over here."

"We got one last shot," Josh reminded everyone. He picked the smallest tater tot from his plate and looked across the table. Staring into Aidan's wide-open mouth, Josh felt like a dentist. He steadied his hand and let the tater tot fly.

It was—good! Aidan closed his mouth and punched his fist into the air. "Dee-licious!" he declared, chewing the winning tater tot.

"Another United victory!" Josh turned to Chris and said, "I'm telling you, these team-building exercises are working. Big time."

Chapter 14

A ll right," Coach Hodges called. "Bring it in." Despite the order, the United players kept playing. Evan slid a back pass to Aidan, who lofted a pass to Josh, positioned perfectly in front of the goal. Josh headed the ball and it looked good, but the ball sailed just inches above the goal. He threw his head back and shouted, "Aaarrgh!"

"Good try," Evan said. "That was *almost* an unbelievable shot."

Evan pointed at Aidan. "Great pass," he said.

The boys turned toward Coach Hodges at the edge of the practice field. A large canvas bag was on the ground next to her.

"Get some water and get over here," she ordered. "Let's hustle."

"What have you cooked up for us today, Josh?" Aidan asked between gulps.

"I didn't cook up anything. But I'm sure someone did," Josh said. He was thinking how much things had changed in such a short time. In the last two weeks, the United had notched two more wins. The team was playing much better—more together. Coach ended every practice with a team-building exercise, and everyone was getting in on it. At the last practice, Kadir led them in an exercise where the players had to lead a blindfolded teammate through an obstacle course using nothing but voice commands.

"Okay, let's get started," Coach said. She pulled away a large cloth cover from the bag and revealed a bunch of brightly colored balloons.

Josh laughed. "Is it your birthday or something, Coach?"

"I hope you brought cake," Aidan added.

Coach Hodges smiled. "No, it's not my birthday. But this could be a good party game." She pointed at Evan. "How about demonstrating this one? Since this was your idea."

Josh and Aidan looked at Evan. "Your idea?"

"Yeah, my idea," Evan said. "I wanted to make sure we didn't have to be blindfolded again. That was scary."

Coach picked a red balloon from the jumble and nodded toward Evan.

"Okay," he said, addressing the team. "The object of the game is to keep the balloon in the air by tapping it."

"With our feet?" Victor asked.

"You can use your hands or feet," he said. "Just don't let the balloon touch the ground."

"Ready?" Coach asked.

"Ready," replied Evan.

Coach tossed the balloon into the air. Evan moved under the balloon as it floated down and easily kept it in the air with a series of hand taps. "Once you get one balloon going," Evan explained as he kept the red balloon aloft with quick taps, "we add another balloon."

Right on cue, Coach tossed another balloon—a green one—into the air. Moving quickly, Evan kept the two balloons in the air for a short while. Soon, however, the balloons drifted apart and one settled onto the grass.

"It's a little harder with two, isn't it?" Coach smiled.

"Yeah. You can't do it alone," Evan said. "So each time Coach tosses in another balloon, someone else needs to come up and help."

"I'll go first," Josh said.

"I'll go next," said Patrick.

"Okay, everybody else line up and get ready," Coach said. "When I toss in a second balloon, Josh will go in to help. When I toss in a third balloon, Patrick will go in. We'll keep adding balloons and teammates."

"Yeah, the idea is to keep as many balloons in the air as we can—together—as a team," Evan said.

"What happens if one touches the ground?" Kadir asked.

"The team loses and we start over again."

"How do we win?" Demetrius asked.

"If we get all eighteen players on the field keeping eighteen balloons up in the air, that's a win," Evan said.

Coach Hodges pulled the bag of balloons next to her. "Okay, let's get started. And remember: talk to each other."

Soon the air was filled with green, yellow, red, and blue balloons. The United players scrambled around the field, tipping them into the air and shouting to each other.

"Watch out for the blue one!"

"I got that red one!"

"Come on, Aidan! Knock 'em higher in the air."

After a few losses, the team started working together, and all eighteen players were moving around the field, calling to each other.

"I've got this one."

"Heads up over there!"

"This one is coming your way!"

Eighteen balloons danced in the soft autumn afternoon.

"Here's another!" Coach shouted as she

tossed still another balloon into the happy mix of players.

The balloons stayed up. All nineteen.

"Here's another. Keep talking to each other."

Twenty!

"Another."

Twenty-one!

One balloon, unnoticed at the edge of the field, floated dangerously close to the ground. Josh leaped for it like a goalkeeper trying desperately to make a save. The balloon bounced off his fingertips and fell to the grass.

Josh rolled onto his back and screamed at the sky. "Aaarrgh!"

"All right. Twenty-one, that's a big win. That's enough for today," Coach said. "You guys did a good job talking to each other. That's the idea. Bring that talking to your teammates to the pitch on Saturday."

"Hey, Coach. What do we do with all of these balloons?" Aidan asked.

"Pop 'em. But be sure to pick up all the pieces."

The team gleefully stomped on the balloons with their cleats.

Pop!

Pop!

Pop!

After picking up the balloon remains, the United players walked toward the parking lot, still laughing and talking.

"Remember, we have the Columbus Day tournament this weekend," Coach Hodges called after them. "I'll e-mail everyone."

Josh walked with Aidan, Evan, and several other United players. "That was an awesome exercise, Evan," he said. Then Josh stopped as if he had forgotten something. He turned to the field.

"Hey, Coach!" Josh shouted.

Coach Hodges looked up.

"Happy Birthday!"

Josh, Aidan, and Evan, along with several other United players, stared up at the big Columbus Day tournament board.

"I can't wait to see our score posted," Kadir said.

"Yeah. I want everybody to see this one!" Mario said. "Three to nothing. We totally dominated!"

Patrick pointed. "Hey, look. They're putting up our score now."

"Way to go, United!" Josh shouted. The United players traded fist bumps and high fives.

"Man, we were scoring like crazy," Evan remembered. "I thought Aidan might even put one in from midfield."

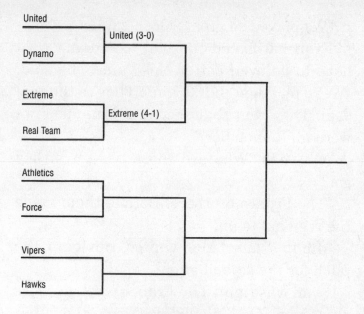

United

United (3-0)

Dynamo

Extreme

Extreme (4-1)

Real Team

Athletics

Force

Vipers

Hawks

"Okay, that's enough celebrating. It's just one game," Coach Hodges said from behind the group. "Our next game is in one hour. Looks like we're playing the Extreme. Rest up and be back here in forty minutes."

"Forty minutes?" Josh repeated. "I guess we're not in the losers bracket anymore."

In no time, Josh was back at the field playing soccer tennis with Aidan, Evan, and two other United players. They were still talking about the United's 3–0 win.

"We played so great," Josh said.

Evan left-footed the ball to Aidan. "We'll have to be even better this game," he said. "We're playing the Extreme. They're the real deal. They won that second tournament we were in. Remember?"

"Oh yeah. Who are those two guys they got?"

"The Franco brothers. Both of them made the regional team."

Minutes later, the United ran onto the pitch for the second game.

Evan was right. The Franco brothers were *very* good. One played forward, the other played center midfield. They controlled the early play with their lightning moves and quick passes. Soon, the Extreme were threatening the United goal.

"Help out. Drop back!" Coach shouted, pumping the palm of her hand in the direction of the United goal.

Josh could see Aidan and the other United defenders struggling to keep up with the Franco brothers. He moved deeper into United's defensive zone.

Just then, Evan darted out and intercepted a crossing pass. The United midfielder pressed the advantage by passing to Josh on the wing. Josh dribbled a short distance, then skipped a pass back to Evan sprinting upfield. Evan broke into the clear. The last Extreme defender scrambled to cover him.

Evan blasted a shot, low and hard, at the far post. The Extreme goalkeeper leaped and knocked it away with a desperate fist-punch.

Evan's run, shot, and near goal made the Extreme more cautious. They hung back on defense for the remainder of the half as the United pressed the attack. The score was tied 0–0 at halftime.

Aidan flopped back on to the grass. "Those Franco brothers are beasts on the field," he said, trying to catch his breath. "At least you guys got that run near the end of the half. That took some of the pressure off."

Evan leaned toward Aidan. "I remember the older brother—the guy playing forward—from the regional team tryouts," he said. "Listen, here's what you've got to do with him." Aidan was all ears as Evan continued. "You got to crowd him, play him real tight. He gets frustrated if he doesn't get the ball with some room. One more thing—overplay him to the right. He loves to go to the right."

Aidan took Evan's advice and played the older Franco tight and tough in the second half. Unable to get his own shot, the older brother laid off a pass for his younger brother midway through the second half.

With a quick touch and a quicker step, the Extreme midfielder created enough space to bend a perfect shot into the upper corner of the United goal. It happened so quickly that Patrick, the United keeper, didn't have time to react. He stood flatfooted on the goal line.

Goal! The United were behind, 1–0.

Wow, those Franco brothers are incredible, Josh thought.

After the goal, the Extreme began to play it safe and fall back on defense. They looked happy, almost relieved, to hold on to their one-goal lead.

The United went on the attack with a series of quick passes at midfield. Evan dribbled forward, charging hard to the top of the box. An Extreme defender challenged him with a skidding tackle.

The referee blew his whistle and reached into his shirt pocket.

A yellow card!

The United had a free kick near the top of the box. Evan spun a dangerous ball toward the right side of the Extreme goal. Sensing the curve of the ball, Josh raced to the spot, got his foot on the ball just in time, and redirected it toward the goal. The ball flew by the Extreme keeper and into the net!

Goal! It was 1–1. Tie game.

The entire team crowded around Josh in celebration.

"Let's get another!" Josh shouted.

The two teams battled hard. Aidan marked the older Franco brother close, sticking to him like a second skin. Finally, the star forward threw his arms up in frustration.

"Come on!" he shouted at his teammates. "Get me the ball."

With Aidan blanketing their best player, the Extreme fell apart.

The United controlled the ball and the play. They filled the pitch with passes and shouts of encouragement.

"Pass back!"

"Look up. On your right."

"Start it over."

"Keep it moving!"

"Josh is open. On the right."

"Cross it."

Josh floated a crossing pass toward the front of the Extreme goal. The keeper rushed out and tried to grab it but got stuck in a tangle of players.

The ball bounced loose. A foot flashed forward in the confusion. The ball flew into the net.

Goal! The United were ahead, 2–1.

"Who scored the goal?" Evan asked as the team jumped up and down together.

"Who cares?" Josh howled. "*We* scored."

The team held on for the 2–1 win. All the United players and fans went wild.

"All right!" Coach Hodges bellowed above

the cheering players and parents. "We're going to the finals!"

"We're in the super-winners bracket!" Josh yelled to Aidan.

Coach held her hands above her head for silence. "The finals are at noon tomorrow," she announced. "We'll have a late breakfast at the motel. Any questions?"

"Yes," Josh dad's said. Everyone looked toward him. "Where are we all going to eat dinner tonight?"

"Yeah. Let's celebrate!!!" Victor shouted.

The United players and parents again burst into cheers.

Chapter 16

Good, you're all here," Coach Hodges said as she came into the breakfast room at the motel.

The United players pushed a group of tables together to crowd around their coach. The parents, who had been drinking coffee and talking soccer, moved closer and stood in a quiet semicircle near the coach and her players.

"Listen up," Coach started. "The team we're playing today—the Vipers—are very good. They have Ricky Abu at center midfield and a bunch of other outstanding players."

"Abu is OD," Evan whispered to Josh.

"What's that?"

"Olympic Development."

"Wow!"

"So we're going to have to play sixty minutes—together," Coach continued, "to beat them."

The moment Josh saw the Vipers warming up, he knew they would be tough. They moved through their passing drills with the breezy confidence of a pro or top college team.

"Is number 10 Abu?" Josh asked Evan.

"Yeah."

Josh nodded. "I figured."

The referee blew his whistle and the teams got ready for the championship game. The Vipers started fast, keeping possession and staying a half step ahead of the scrambling United. Patrick made several saves to keep the United in the game. But he didn't have a chance when Abu spun free near the goal and left-footed a shot into the upper corner.

Goal!

The Vipers had jumped on top 1–0.

But unlike early in the season, the United

did not give up. They got possession and then got lucky.

Victor sailed a crossing pass from the left wing toward the front of the Vipers goal. Josh leaped up in a crowd of Viper and United players. The ball banged against the side of Josh's head and ricocheted off a defender's leg—past the stunned Vipers goalkeeper—and into the net.

Goal! A lucky goal. But still a goal.

The score was tied 1–1.

"That's your goal," Aidan said, pointing to Josh as the team celebrated.

Josh shook his head.

"It is," Evan insisted. "You were the last guy on our team to touch it."

Josh smiled. "It's *our* goal."

The score stayed tied deep into the second half. The Vipers and their star midfielder controlled play. Josh could sense the United hanging on, almost hoping for a tie.

Late in the half, Abu spun past Aidan, who was marking him closely, and sprinted toward the goal. Demetrius, the other United defender, raced over and took Abu down with a hard tackle just as he crossed into the penalty area.

Tweeeeeeeeeeeet! The referee held up a red card.

A penalty kick.

The United were down a man. Demetrius was out of the game.

"Maybe he'll miss," Josh whispered to Evan as the teams got behind the penalty line and Abu got ready to kick.

"No chance," Evan said.

Evan was right. No chance. Abu drilled the kick into the left corner.

The United were now behind 2–1.

Coach made some changes, substituting in fresh players for tired ones.

"Five minutes to go!" Coach shouted from the sidelines. "Give it everything you've got. Take some chances. Go for the goal."

The United kept hustling, but Josh could feel the game slipping away. Up a player, the Vipers skillfully kept possession and the ball in the United zone.

Just when time was running out and any chance of tying the game was slipping away,

Aidan stole a pass and charged upfield. He saw Josh racing up the right side and angled a perfect pass to him.

This may be our last run, Josh thought, stopping the ball with a quick touch and sizing up his next move. He spotted Evan in the center, sent the ball to him with a swift kick, and kept running. Evan dribbled around a Viper defender and skidded a pass back to Josh advancing past midfield. Josh back passed to Aidan, hustling after the play with Viper forwards trailing him.

The United kept passing the ball faster and faster.

To Evan.

To Josh.

To Aidan.

Then back to Josh, who was open on the wing. *Last chance*, he thought as he sent the ball spinning toward the goal.

The Vipers goalkeeper was ready. He crashed into the crowd of players and fisted the ball.

Still running upfield, Aidan met the bouncing ball near the top of the penalty area. With a quick touch of his right foot, he lofted it back toward the goal.

Josh, Evan, and a cluster of the Vipers watched as the ball floated over the goalkeeper and slipped under the crossbar, into the net.

Goal! The score was tied, 2–2.

A minute later, the referee blew his whistle and the game was over. Or was it? The referee called the two coaches over to the sidelines.

"What's happening?" Aidan asked as the coaches and referee talked. "Are we playing overtime?"

"I don't know," Josh said. "Maybe it's a tie."

"No way," Evan said, shaking his head. "This is a big tournament."

Coach came back to the team. She was smiling. "Penalty kicks," she announced. "Best of five kicks."

"Who's gonna take the kicks?" Josh asked above the noise.

Coach studied her clipboard for a moment. "Okay, let's have…

Victor.

Aidan.

Kadir.

Josh.

And Evan."

Coach pressed into the circle of five players moving nervously about, getting ready for their penalty kicks. "Pick a spot," she instructed. "Don't look at the keeper. Just pick a spot and let it go."

All the players on the field got behind the penalty line.

The United goalkeeper and Vipers first shooter looked lonely as the shooter set the ball on a spot ten yards in front of the goal and got ready to kick.

It's a big net. It's an easy shot, Josh thought, trying to psych himself up for his turn. *Of course, that's why everybody expects you to make it!*

"Hey," Evan said, getting the attention of all the United players. "Hook 'em."

Without a word, the United players locked elbows.

The Vipers shooter drove the ball into the corner.

1–0.

Victor did the same.

1–1.

The next four kicks were all good. The score was 3–3.

The Vipers were up again. This time Patrick, the United goalkeeper, guessed right. He dove straight out to the left and knocked the Vipers shot away.

It was still 3–3 and Josh had a chance to put the United in the lead.

Josh placed the ball down on the spot. He stepped back slowly, counting his steps and trying to breathe deeply.

His mind was racing. *Don't aim too high. Don't look at the keeper. Just hit it solid.*

Josh took one last deep breath. He stepped forward, keeping his head down. He felt a tingling sensation streak through his body as his right foot hit the ball—solidly. He looked up and saw the ball leap into the back of the net.

The United were ahead, 4–3.

But not for long. Abu coolly tied the score again with a low blast that grazed the inside of the post.

4–4.

It was all up to Evan. Standing back with teammates, Josh locked arms with Kadir and Aidan. "Come on, Evan," he whispered under his breath.

Josh was almost afraid to look, but he had to. He saw Evan drive forward and the Vipers goalkeeper leap, anticipating the direction of Evan's shot. At the last instant, Evan hooked the ball in the other direction, bouncing it into the other side of the goal.

Evan turned to his teammates and raised his arms high above his head in the shape of a V for Victory: 5–4 in penalty kicks!

In a flash, the players ran together. Evan, Josh, and Aidan were at the center of the happy United players.

The tournament-champion United.

The six-wins-in-a-row United.

The new United.

Chapter 17

There he is," Josh said, pointing to the cabin near the entrance of High-Top Park. "Come on."

Josh and Aidan waved goodbye to Josh's father and walked quickly across the parking lot toward the cabin. Evan greeted his teammates with tight handgrips and quick shoulder bumps.

"That guy Berkeley is here again today," Evan said. "Let's get going. We got a lot of climbing to do."

Berkeley smiled when he saw the three boys in their United jerseys. "Hey, it's the soccer guys. How's the team doing?"

"A lot better," Josh said. "We've won six games in a row."

"We even won a tournament over the Columbus Day weekend," Evan added.

"Evan scored the game winner," Aidan said, trying to lift his teammate's arm in triumph. "We won on penalty kicks."

"Whoa...sounds like you guys are doing a lot better than the last time I saw you," Berkeley said. "Maybe that climbing session did the trick."

"And all the team-building stuff Josh started," Aidan added.

"Hey, what about me?" Evan protested. "I came up with the balloon game. I thought that was awesome."

"What about Ms. Littlewood?" Josh said. "If she hadn't assigned that research project, we wouldn't have found out about the 1999 Women's World Cup Team."

"I don't know what you guys are talking about," Berkeley said. "But never mind. Let's get started." Berkeley looked over the boys' heads. "Where's the rest of the team?"

"It's just the three of us," Josh explained. "We figured this would be a fun thing to do together."

Berkeley again reviewed the safety rules of the park as the boys stepped into their climbing harnesses and fastened all the clips. "It's a double-clip system. There's no way you can fall. There should only be one guy on an element at a time. Stay away from the diamond and double-diamond courses."

"We did the blue course last time," Josh said. "Which course should we try this time?"

Berkeley thought for a moment. "Follow the green course. It's got a long zip line in the middle. I think you guys will like it."

The three boys scrambled up the wide log ladder leading to the large platform that looked like a tree house. Josh looked out from the platform. The October leaves were beginning to fall. They sifted through the cool air and settled silently on the ground.

"There's the first element on the green course," Evan said. "I'll go first."

"I got second," Aidan called.

Josh smiled. "I guess I'm last."

The boys started off, climbing up rope ladders higher into the trees and across bridges made of swinging logs. After about twenty minutes they stopped on a platform and caught their breath.

"Here's the zip line Berkeley told us about," Josh said. A long cable stretched tight from their platform to another one some distance away.

"It's so far across, I can hardly see the other platform," Aidan said.

Josh glanced at Evan. "You still want to go first?"

"No problem." Evan attached his harness to the zip line, took a deep breath, and grabbed onto the top knob that moved along the line. "Here goes nothing," he said as he pushed off the platform.

"Yeeooooowwwweeee!"

As soon as Evan swung onto the far platform, he turned and called back, "Berkeley was right—this is great!"

A minute later, Aidan was with Evan, and Josh stood alone on his platform, staring at the long silent wire. He attached his harness to the zip line, grabbed onto the top knob, and stepped off.

The speed of the zip line surprised Josh.

The trees and branches rushed by in a blur of color. *This is a lot faster than the blue course*, he thought. Josh tightened his hands on the top knob. He didn't mean to, but he triggered the brake system. The knob pressed against the wire and he came to a stop about ten yards short of the platform. Josh, still attached to the wire, dangled in the air. His heart jumped.

Don't look down, he thought. *Remember what Berkeley said: "There's no way to fall."*

Josh stared at Aidan and Evan. They looked awfully far away.

"You can move forward by pulling on the wire!" Evan shouted. "Hand over hand, like this." Evan and Aidan reached their hands over their heads and demonstrated how it was done.

Josh looked at the zip line above his head and began to pull at it with his hands. Slowly he began to inch forward. Closer...closer... closer to the platform. Evan and Aidan cheered him on.

"Come on, you can do it."

"Keep pulling."

As he neared the platform, Josh let go of the wire. His teammates, still clipped to a safety line, were leaning out from the platform with their hands extended. Josh reached for them, and Evan and Aidan grabbed his wrists and pulled him up. The boys traded high fives. Josh stood there for a moment, looking around at the trees—the red, yellow, and orange fall leaves—and his teammates. He thought about how the United season had turned around, how the United had really become a team.

Josh let his breath out in a rush and said, "I guess this is another win for the United."

The Real Story

Ms. Littlewood was right; the 1999 United States Women's World Cup soccer team was loaded with talent. Three Hall of Fame players led this extraordinary team:

Mia Hamm was a high-scoring star of four national championship teams at the University of North Carolina (UNC). She scored 158 goals in international matches, a record for men and women.

Michelle Akers was a dominating midfielder who had starred in college at the University of Central Florida. As strong a player as she was, though, Akers suffered from chronic fatigue syndrome, a condition that left her exhausted after matches.

Kristine Lilly, Mia Hamm's teammate at UNC, was a versatile forward and midfielder. She set a record for playing in 352 international matches.

But that wasn't all. The team had Brandi Chastain, Carla Overbeck, and Joy Fawcett on defense and Briana Scurry in the goal. Julie Foudy played in the midfield and Tiffeny Milbrett played up front. There were so many outstanding players that All-Americans such as Shannon MacMillan from the University of Portland found it hard to get playing time.

Despite having an equally talented team (including many of the 1999 players), the 1995 U.S. team had failed to win the World Cup. That year, the U.S. women lost a heartbreaking game to Norway in the semifinals, 1–0.

When the U.S. team began training for the 1999 World Cup tournament, they knew they had to try something different to give them an edge in close games. So head Coach Tony DiCicco decided to hire sports psychologist Colleen Hacker to help the players with their mental game, according to Jere Longman, author of *The Girls of Summer*.

During her time as a soccer coach at Pacific Lutheran University, Hacker had led her team to three national titles in the National Association of Intercollegiate Athletics (NAIA), an organization of smaller colleges.

Hacker knew that the U.S. team already had terrific athletes. "My goal isn't to fix problem athletes," she said, according to Longman. "My ultimate goal is to take excellence and eke out a little more."

The U.S. players had come together from different teams. Hacker wanted to get them to connect with one another and play together like a seasoned team. For example, when the team went on the road trips, she made sure the players changed roommates. That way, the players got to know different teammates better and didn't just hang out with the same ones.

Hacker also led the players in team-building exercises similar to the ones Josh's United team did. In one exercise, she had players lead their teammates down a 600-foot cliff—blindfolded! The team-building exercises helped the players work together as a team, communicate with one another, and support each other when things went against them.

All the practice and team-building exercises paid off in the 1999 World Cup tournament. The U.S. team rolled through their first round of games (the Group stage), easily beating Denmark (3–0), Nigeria (7–1), and North Korea (3–0). The games were played in front of huge, enthusiastic crowds in New York, Chicago, and Boston. America was getting very excited about their team.

But winning a World Cup is never easy. In the first five minutes of the quarterfinal game against Germany—a game the U.S. had to win to stay in the running for the World Cup—Brandi Chastain accidentally knocked the ball into her own goal. The U.S. was behind, 1–0.

But Brandi's teammates did not criticize Brandi for her costly mistake. Instead, Carla Overbeck, the team captain, went over to her and, according to Longman, said, "This game is not over. There are 85 minutes left. We are going to win this thing. Don't worry about it."

The U.S. team came back—scoring three goals, including one by Brandi Chastain—to beat Germany, 3–2.

After defeating Brazil 2–0, the U.S. team was ready to play China in the finals. The game was going to be a tough one. China's team—led by forward Sun Wen, one of the best players in the world—had crushed Norway 5–0 in the other semifinal.

More than 90,000 fans packed the sun-drenched Rose Bowl in Pasadena, California, on July 10, 1999. Millions more watched on televisions all over the country.

The teams battled hard for two 45-minute halves in the 100-degree heat. Michelle Akers became so exhausted she had to leave the game. Akers listened to the rest of the game in a medical room underneath the Rose Bowl.

Neither team could get a ball into the net. The score was tied, 0–0, after the second half and the game went into a 15-minute over-time.

China almost ended the game during overtime on a header off a corner kick. The ball sailed toward the U.S. net, but Kristine Lilly, standing just inches from the goal line, headed the ball away. The ball bounced dangerously in front of the U.S. net until Brandi Chastain booted it away.

No score. The teams played a second 15-minute overtime. Again, no goals. So the World Cup—just like the United's big game against the Vipers—had to be decided on penalty kicks.

Just like Coach Hodges, Coach DiCicco had to decide which five players would take the all-important kicks. He chose these women for the crucial kicks:

Carla Overbeck.

Joy Fawcett.

Kristine Lilly.

Mia Hamm.

And Brandi Chastain.

Overbeck and Fawcett drilled their kicks into the net. But so did the first two Chinese players. On the third Chinese kick, U.S. goalkeeper Briana Scurry leaped to her left and stretched her body out as far as she could. The ball glanced off her fingertips and away from the net.

No goal!

Kristine Lilly and Mia Hamm came through for their team by blasting their kicks into the net. But again, the Chinese players converted their penalty kicks. The score was 4–4 in penalty kicks. It was all up to Brandi Chastain.

She took a deep breath, stepped forward, and powered a shot into the back of the net.

The United States had won!

They won the World Cup because they were more than just a group of All-Stars. They were a real team.

About the Author

Fred Bowen was a Little Leaguer who loved to read. Now he is the author of many action-packed books of sports fiction. He has also written a weekly sports column for kids in The *Washington Post* since 2000.

Fred played lots of sports growing up, including soccer at Marblehead High School. For thirteen years, he coached kids' baseball, soccer, and basketball teams. Some of his stories spring directly from his coaching experience and his sports-happy childhood in Marblehead, Massachusetts.

Fred holds a degree in history from the University of Pennsylvania and a law degree from George Washington University. He was a lawyer for many years before retiring to become a full-time children's author. Bowen has been a guest author at schools and conferences across the country, as well as the Smithsonian Institute in Washington, DC, and The Baseball Hall of Fame.

Fred lives in Silver Spring, Maryland, with his wife Peggy Jackson. They have two grown children.

www.fredbowen.com

Acknowledgments

Much of the information about the 1999 United States Women's World Cup soccer team comes from the book, *The Girls of Summer: The U.S. Women's Soccer Team and How It Changed the World,* by Jere Longman (Harper Perennial, 2001). I also used the websites www.wikipedia.com and www.fifa.com.

I would also like to thank the following people for their help:

Colleen M. Hacker, Ph.D., Professor of Movement Studies and Wellness Education at Pacific Lutheran University in Tacoma, Washington. Professor Hacker, who was a mental skills coach to the 1999 Women's World Cup team, was kind enough to speak to me about the 1999 team and the team-building exercises that were so helpful in winning the World Cup.

Berkeley Williams, park manager at The Adventure Park at Sandy Spring Friends School in Sandy Spring, Maryland. Berkeley was nice enough to show me around The Adventure Park and explain what was going on in the treetops.

HEY, SPORTS FANS!

Don't miss these action-packed books by Fred Bowen...

Real Hoops
PB: $5.95 / 978-1-56145-566-9 / 1-56145-566-0
Hud can run, pass, and shoot at top speed. But he's not much of a team player. Can Ben convince Hud to leave his dazzling—but one-man—style back on the asphalt?

Quarterback Season
PB: $5.95 / 978-1-56145-594-2 / 1-56145-594-6
Matt expects to be the starting quarterback. But after a few practices watching Devro, a talented seventh grader, he's starting to get nervous. To make matters worse, his English teacher is on his case about a new class assignment: a journal.

Go for the Goal!
PB: $5.95 / 978-1-56145-632-1 / 1-56145-632-2
Josh and his talented travel league soccer teammates are having trouble coming together as a successful team—until he convinces them to try team-building exercises.

Perfect Game (coming Spring 2013)
PB: $5.95 / 978-1-56145-625-3 / 1-56145-5625-X
Isaac is a perfectionist, especially when it comes to baseball. When things go wrong on the field, he is too quick to lose his temper. Can working with a soccer team of developmentally challenged and mainstream kids help Isaac learn to control his meltdowns?

Check out **www.SportsStorySeries.com** for more info.

Want more?

All-St⭐r Sports Story
Series

All-Star Sports Story Series

T. J.'s Secret Pitch
PB: $5.95 / 978-1-56145-504-1 / 1-56145-504 0

T. J.'s pitches just don't pack the power to strike out the batters, but the story of 1940s baseball hero Rip Sewell and his legendary eephus pitch may help him find a solution.

The Golden Glove
PB: $5.95 / 978-1-56145-505-8 / 1 56145-505-9

Without his lucky glove, Jamie doesn't believe in his ability to lead his baseball team to victory. How will he learn that faith in oneself is the most important equipment for any game?

The Kid Coach
PB: $5.95 / 978-1-56145-506-5 / 1-56145-506-7

Scott and his teammates can't find an adult to coach their team, so they must find a leader among themselves.

Playoff Dreams
PB: $5.95 / 978-1-56145-507-2 / 1-56145-507-5

Brendan is one of the best players in the league, but no matter how hard he tries, he can't make his team win.

Winners Take All
PB: $5.95 / 978-1-56145-512-6 / 1-56145-512-1

Kyle makes a poor decision to cheat in a big game. Someone discovers the truth and threatens to reveal it. What can Kyle do now?

All-St★r Sports Story
Series